A Poet's Bird Garden

Laura Nyman Montenegro

Farrar Straus Giroux • New York

For Olga Gluck, my grandmother

Distributed in Canada by Douglas & McIntyre Ltd.

Color separations by Chroma Graphics PTE Ltd.

Printed and bound in the United States of America by Phoenix Color Corporation

Designed by Robbin Gourley

First edition, 2007

10   9   8   7   6   5   4   3   2   1

www.fsgkidsbooks.com

Library of Congress Cataloging-in-Publication Data

Montenegro, Laura Nyman.

    A poet's bird garden / Laura Nyman Montenegro.— 1st ed.

      p.   cm.

    Summary: After Chirpie the bird escapes from her cage and flies into a tree, a
group of poets decides that the best way to entice her down is to create a garden
full of seeds, water, hiding places, and materials for building a nest.

    ISBN-13: 978-0-374-36038-2

    ISBN-10: 0-374-36038-3

    [1. Birds—Fiction.   2. Poets—Fiction.   3. Gardens—Fiction.   4. Stories in
rhyme.]   I. Title.

PZ8.3.M7746 Poe 2007

[E]—dc22

                                               2005056810

I open the door to Chirpie's cage and

she flies straight to the branch of a tree.

I run to tell Monica.
She calls the poets.
"Natalie's bird is out," she says.
"We need you to come RIGHT AWAY."

The poets arrive. I open the gate. Priyanka says,
"I've brought Vincent, Lily, and Pendleton, too,
and Marion is coming—she's tying her shoe.
You need not worry. Haven't you heard?
There are oodles of ways to lure a bird."

"Stand still like a statue and Chirpie will come sit on your shoulder," coos Priyanka.

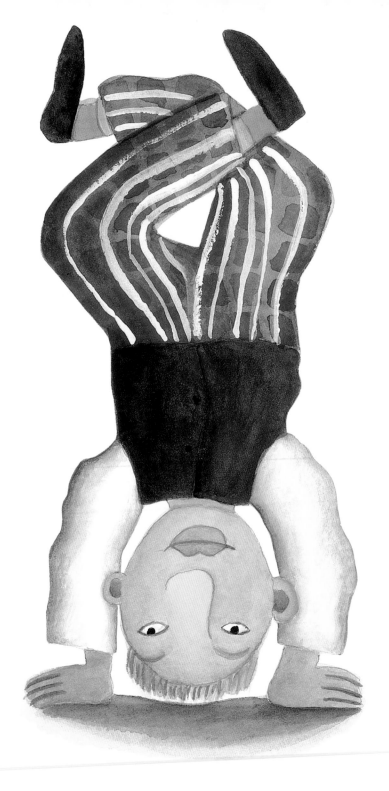

"Wiggle like a worm: it's a trick that's much older," warbles Vincent.

"Sing like a bird and make a happy melody," twitters Lily.

"When she gets homesick, she'll come down from the tree," clucks Pendleton.

Then Marion steps forward.
"Excuse me, dear poets,
may I make a motion?
Be still, close your eyes,
hear the following notion.
We must try to imagine
the mind of the bird,
complex and quick-witted,
quite brilliant, I've heard.
If I were Chirpie,
fancy and free,
what beauty would beckon me
down from the tree?
A garden, my friends,
made especially for birds,
a poet's bird garden
too lovely for words.
We must get started."

Marion tells them:
"The first thing we do to fulfill the bird's needs
is give her some pumpkin and cantaloupe seeds."
Pendleton serves seeds for lunch.

NO CHIRPIE.

"A bird must have water, tranquil and cool,
for drinking and bathing, a shimmering pool."
Priyanka brings water and fills the bowls.

STILL NO CHIRPIE.

"Give Chirpie a bush in which to hide,
a thicket of tangles, an oasis inside."
Lily and Vincent dig a hole and plant a bush.

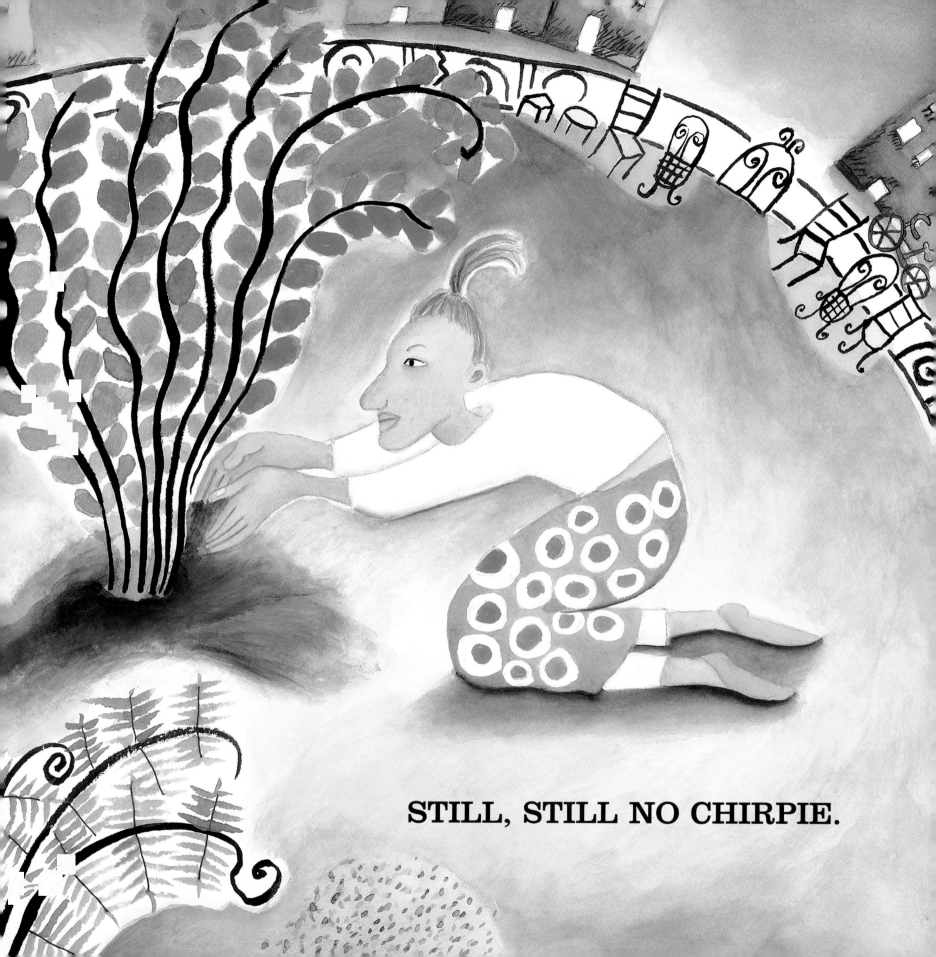

STILL, STILL NO CHIRPIE.

"A bird loves to build a beautiful nest.
String and yarn make a soft place to rest."
I run to get an old sweater to unravel, and Monica and I
hang bits of yarn and string all around the garden.

CHIRPIE, COME DOWN!

"And last of all, poets, the most difficult feat:
Don't whisper, don't wiggle. You must stay in your seats.
The bird's favorite places are quiet and still."
We sit quietly.
And wait.
And wait.
And wait.
AND WAIT.

Finally, Vincent stands up.

"Enough!" he shouts. "That's it. Now I know it.

You shouldn't have left this up to poets.

I'm going home, and I beg your pardon,

but not ONE BIRD has come to our magnificent garden."

"UH-OH," says Priyanka, "Chirpie's not in the tree.
She was just there—now where can she be?
Shh, I hear rustling under the ferns.
Could that be CHIRPIE searching for worms?"

AHA!
It's not Chirpie!
IT'S CLAUDE.

"Get out of the garden, Claude, out on the double.
YOU are the reason we're having this trouble!"

Look! Here they come.
That's oh, SO MUCH better.

And look who's got a piece of my sweater!
Chirpie's come down, she's come down from the tree.
Tee-tilly, twee-tilly,
tipi-to-wee.